Warner Juvenile Books Edition

Warner Books, Inc., 666 Fifth Avenue, New York, NY 10103
A Warner Communications Company

Printed in the United States of America
First Warner Juvenile Books Printing: March 1988
10 9 8 7 6 5 4 3 2 1

Library of Congress Cataloging-in-Publication Data

Gilchrist, Guy.
Tiny dinos ABC.

Summary: In this rhyming story, tiny dinosaurs describe their favorite things, from A (Airplane) to Z (Zebra).

[1. Alphabet. 2. Dinosaurs—Fiction. 3. Stories in rhyme] I. Title.
PZ8.3.G39Ti 1988 [E] 87-40336
ISBN 1-55782-012-0

THIS ABC IS FOR A.B.S.

Guy Gilchrist's

Tiny Dinos ABC

WARNER JUVENILE BOOKS
A Warner Communications Company
NEW YORK

A is for the **A**irplane
that wakes the Tiny Dinos up.

B is for a **B**owl of **B**ananas,
C's for **C**ake and **C**up.

D stands for **D**ino…

and **D**iaper…

and **D**ish.

E's the **E**ggs that Rex would eat
if he could have his wish!

F is for **F**rog, **F**lowers,
Foot and **F**ruit.
A **G**reen **G**uitar starts with **G**.
(Did you hear something toot?)

A **H**orn! **H**orn starts with **H**,
like **H**armonica and **H**ats.
Tiny Dinos sing and play!
Wow! They're going bats!

I is for **I**ce cream
that tastes good
in the heat.

A **J**ar of **J**elly
starts with **J**.
(That's what Rex
would like to eat!)

K is for **K**ite and
Kitten, and also
stands for **K**ey.
Looks like **K**itty
likes to sleep on
Baby Bronty's **K**nee!

L is for **L**obster,
tasty with **L**emon or **L**ime.
Milk begins with **M**.
Hey, Rex, that **M**ilk is mine!

N stands for **N**uts that you
can balance on your **N**ose.
(It's hard to do if you're
a Dino standing on your toes!)

O's for the **O**range **O**ctopus,
sleeping on an **O**ar.

A **P**ile of
Pineapples
begins with **P**.
(Hear Rex's stomach roar?)

Q stands for our lovely **Q**ueen,
lying on her **Q**uilt.
R is for **R**ocks –
and a **R**ed **R**aft Sir Waldo built.

S stands for **S**ky,
Starfish, **S**hell and **S**and.

T's the **T**urtle
Tap dancing in Tiny Ptery's hand.

U is for **U**mbrella,
when the island rain is pouring down.
V's for the **V**egetables
drinking rain that hits the ground.

W is for **W**ater and
Whale and
Words galore!

X is for **X**ylophone
and really not much more.

Y is for **Y**ellow
egg **Y**olks making
messy gook!

Z is for the
Zebra saying,
"Zat's Zee end of Zis book!"

THE JOLLY TURTLE